SEVERANCE

SEVERANCE

stories

ROBERT OLEN BUTLER

CHRONICLE BOOKS
SAN FRANCISCO

With special thanks to Jay Schaefer, Catherine Argand, and
Isabelle Reinharez, and to David Baker, James Cummins,
and David Lehman.

The stories in this book originally appeared in *Agni, The Cincinnati
Review, Five Points, The Georgia Review, Glimmer Train, The Kenyon
Review, McSweeney's, Ninth Letter, Open City, Prairie Schooner,
The Southern Review, Tin House, 21, Virginia Quarterly Review,* and
Water-Stone Review.

Library of Congress Cataloging-in-Publication Data is available.

ISBN-10: 0-8118-5614-3
ISBN-13: 978-0-8118-5614-0

Manufactured in Canada

Designed by Brooke Johnson

Distributed in Canada by Raincoast Books
9050 Shaughnessy Street
Vancouver, British Columbia V6P 6E5

10 9 8 7 6 5 4 3 2 1

Chronicle Books LLC
680 Second Street
San Francisco, California 94107

www.chroniclebooks.com

for **ELIZABETH**

This book began when I showed you my beloved Saigon and
we stood before the guillotine at the War Crimes Museum.
My head was already over my heels for you.

After careful study and due deliberation it is my opinion the head remains conscious for one minute and a half after decapitation.

—DR. DASSY D'ESTAING, 1883

In a heightened state of emotion, we speak at the rate of 160 words per minute.

—DR. EMILY REASONER, *A Sourcebook of Speech,* 1975

MUD

man, beheaded by saber-toothed
tiger, circa 40,000 B.C.

sharp the air with cold that comes so fast, and far we all run, along
water turning to rock, many suns and only short-snout and
short-snout to eat between us, the old of us lagging, the
cold rushing, the touchwood barely warm we blow long on
the touchwood last darktime, we blow and much growling
anger for the touchwood keeps its flame tight, we all will
lose the flame soon, and we alone fall back to the old ones
in skins but we all keep the body-grease for our ourselves to
hold our heat inside while the old carry the cold inside, and
one is the suckle woman, long suns past she holds us alone to
her suckle and we alone sit at flame and suckle woman puts
her hand upon our head alone and puts her mouth to our ear
alone and makes a soft cry, but we all feel the time coming
like many suns past, before suckle woman is old, and there
were other old and the cold came quick and we all were
drawn tight on our bones and the biting was fierce in our
centers and we all were going slow and it was time to eat, to
eat the old, and now the cold is upon us and now the time is
again and we alone fall back to hold the suckle woman and
to make cries into her ear before we all eat

MEDUSA

Gorgon and former human beauty,
beheaded by Perseus, circa 2000 B.C.

dreaming, surely I dream now: I can still shake my hair down long
and billowing like waves upon the sea, how tender I am
how fair I can see in the reflection of water and shield and
a man's eyes, and this softer hair makes no difference I still
turn a man to stone who looks at me, the part of him that
snakes inside me, a clefting of stone, and my body weeps the
sea, pours forth the thickest sea for my god-man Poseidon
who smells of brine and the great swimming creatures who
attend him scaled and heavy wet limbs about me and that
bitch Athena thinks her temple defiled but it was he who
came to me and leaned his trident upon her marble face and
dripped upon her floor, she tries to hurt me but I love my
living hair these serpents whisper when men come close
each strand with a split tongue hissing my desire for them
I shake my dear children my tresses down and they curl
back up their black eyes flashing and the man cries out at my
beauty and then his tongue and face and chest and arms and
thighs and his toad-headed serpent all turn hard forever the
clearing before my cave is thronged with them my admirers,
but my children are my true loves rooted in my brain and
gathered sleeping against my face muttering sibilant dreams
of love

MARCUS TULLIUS
CICERO

orator and politician, beheaded on
orders of Marc Antony, 43 B.C.

louder, Marcus Tullius, I cannot hear you cries Helvia my noble mother
her forehead ringed in curls calling from the top row of the
empty theater *speak louder* and my arms are leaden from a
thousand apt gestures and I cannot think and I am small
stand straight she cries I lift my upper body and the senators
are packed before me like sardelles straight from the sea their
eyes unblinking their mouths gaping my voice rings through
the curia and I feel the comforting press of my toga over my
shoulder and now the senate is empty but for Antony *speak
up* he says *I cannot hear you* his centurions are nowhere in
sight and I straighten and say *if, noble Antony, your nobility were made coinage for the empire its measure would be*—I
falter—I adjust the toga folds about my chest, searching for
an appropriately minuscule measure—but time is running
quickly, I know—I have no arms to lift—*your nobility* I say
*is the nobility of green flies on goat shit they glitter in the sun-
light and they eat and they move their wings and fly but their life
is short* and Antony lifts up on diaphanous wings and rises
and vanishes and now a woman's voice says *speak up, Marcus
Tullius, speak up I cannot hear you* and I say *o noble mother,
Helvia, if your nobility were made coinage for the empire*

JOHN
THE
BAPTIST

prophet, beheaded by
King Herod, circa 30

smelling of garlic he comes to me and he is lank with long hands and I rejoice that he enjoys his food and that in my own mouth there was only the bitter crunch of locust and the sour berry and the cloying of wild honey as I waited for him and I draw my face close to his mouth as I hold him in my arms to smell his very breath and I feel the hardness of his back and his hand curls up to cup my elbow angled by his side I pull that arm closer laying it along his body feeling his ribs and the Jordan rushes about us the fish rubbing at my legs like hungry dogs and I am hungry too and I would rub against him, my Lord my face of God, his eyes dark and narrowing at me as I hesitate to press him under and he whispers to me *John you must do this* and my mouth would speak but it is so close to his now and I lift him slightly toward me this man I have waited for all my life, waited to kiss, thinking it would be his feet but now I would have him open his mouth and devour me take me in his mouth and let me disappear into his very flesh and I would be sweet to his taste I am certain and he says *John*

VALERIA
MESSALINA

wife of Emperor Claudius 1 of Rome,
beheaded by order of her husband, 48

I am sighted through my tongue I run the tip of my tongue through
the cleft of his chin watching him and I hear through my
tongue I draw my tongue across his chest and pause and
listen to his heart beating, rushing faster even as I linger
here, and I lift my face from the chest of my Caius Silius we
are panting now we are the Circus Maximus we are the rush
of wheels the wild breath of horses on the throne room floor
the bright expanse of marble I shift my eyes and I see us both
in the mirror of stone our flanks naked and pressed together
as one I return my eyes to him, his head reclines, he sighs, I
memorize his flesh the faint groove along the underside of
his jaw the marble expanse of his chest this cinnamon nipple
I pluck now with my lips and just below it is the red birth
spot, the kiss of the goddess Voluptas: I have turned my eyes
away from this too long, I will pull down her temple for this,
I draw a circle around this spot on his flesh with my tongue I
take it between my teeth tugging gently and he moans and
I bite hard now his skin yielding his blood sudden and warm
his body thrashes but I hold fast to my man I tear this other
kiss from his body

DIOSCORUS

shipmaster and companion to Paul, beheaded by
Roman soldiers who mistook him for the apostle, 67

sails swell and braces hum overhead, my hand on the tiller night and day and night again and all the things of the world are beneath my feet now, all at once, the timber and the cattle and the linen and the glass, the wine, the wool, ivory and apes, olives and cheese, plums and pears and pomegranates and ginger, myrrh and incense, alabaster and amber, oysters and slaves, their dark eyes turning to me awake in the midst of the night as I hug the coast out of Aden and it's day now and still I have wind in the great middle sea and I have woodwork and statuary from Sicily and papyrus and granite and glass from Egypt, corn and fish and hides from the Black Sea and from Smyrna I have carpets rolled and bound and stacked in the hold, and passengers, a man and two others who bow to him a man with a naked head like mine bare to the sky and the wind, there is only the terrible motionlessness of my house, becalmed, my son barely drawing a breath, this man touches my son's head and speaks to his god and my son lives and the man says *leave all these things* and I am in a marketplace and I cry out the name of this man's god as if into a gale and around me are figs and linen and vessels of clay

PAUL
(SAUL OF TARSUS)

apostle, beheaded
by the Emperor Nero, 67

narrow the gate through to the warren of merchants past figs and linen and clay vessels the smells of wood fire and bodies moving in the shadows of houses I am restless in my limbs and the way turns to a square a fountain and a great and sudden flare of light, I close my eyes to the welter of it blinded and open them again, and in the center of this brilliance a woman young her hair loose radiant her forearms bare she is bent to draw water and she lifts her face to me her eyes dark in the midst of the light which roils silently all about her and within me and I would move to her now and kneel before the mysteries of her body I am tumescent with devotion but instantly she turns her face away and I hesitate gasping waiting, if she but speak if she but call me to her, for all my readiness to act I wait and my horse nickers at my restlessness the land flat to the horizons my body sucked dry by the sun Damascus ahead and heretic Jews to shackle at the wrists at the ankles and the air around me ignites I am at the center of a flame and I am tumbling down I am on my knees I lift my face to see her and instead I hear a voice, a man, and I understand

MATTHEW

tax collector and apostle, beheaded
by King Hirtacus of Ethiopia, 78

faintly bitter, the smell of this wine, the old man stands with eyes rheumy in the shade of my custom shack and he says *please honorable publican this is very low quality wine* and I say *it is wormwood wine which adds twenty-five percent to the value at thirteen percent tax you owe the Empire three drachmas for these goods* and I wait for him to appeal my application of the highest allowed duty and then I will explain the further tax on horse and cart and wheels and the bridge he must cross and I will listen and allow him to convince me to lower the rate of duty by a few points and this will still leave me ample profit my thumb sliding up and down my forefinger on my writing hand I wait and he is silent and beyond him the Sea of Galilee is bright from the sun but it is more than that, the tips of the upchurning waves are flames rising and I begin to tremble and now a day of clouds and a fine misty rain and he says *follow me* and we are at Cana, he and the others he's called and his mother, and there is no wine and he passes his hand over six jugs of water and I sniff there and it is fine aged wine at ten drachmas per jug at thirteen percent duty *be still* he says

VALENTINE

Roman priest and saint, beheaded by
Emperor Claudius II, circa 270

in she pads and crouches over me, quietly, the she-wolf, I am in her
cave, not beneath the fig tree where Romulus and Remus cry
in hunger, she has abandoned them to give me her tit and
the cave is my jail cell and I wake ready to die for my Lord,
His name on my lips, the dream a dream from my childhood
before Christ and I crouch tiny in our doorway and naked
men run by striking the backs of women who willingly bare
their flesh to receive the lash of goatskin, receiving fertility
on the day of Lupercalia, and Julia appears now at my cell
door, daughter of Asterius my jailer, her eyes sightless from
birth, I rise and cross to her and take the cup of water and
the crust of bread and I drop them at once, knowing this
time my hands are filled with the Spirit and I need only
touch her eyelids and she will see, and her hair falls soft
about her shoulders and I hesitate, my loins filling, and in
my head the sound of naked men rushing past and we bare
our backs, we priests, ready for the lash of God, and her face
is lambent, turned slightly aside, and I slough off my clothes:
I am naked, visibly filled with the ache of men, and I lay my
thumbs lightly on her eyes so she can see her Valentine

DRAGON

beast, beheaded by Saint George, 301

fly and land and run upon the pale fleshy jitteries I breathe hot upon them their wailing comes then and in my mouth the soft flail of their limbs the pulpy oozy of them and the cracky breaking, this body I eat nice body, oozy too this blood I drink nice blood, I settle my legs and I fold my wings the quieting comes upon me now after the bodies and the blood, all the rushy sputtery in my center is gone, the flying and landing and running all done, more of the fleshies dashing off I watch them and they seem now much like my eggy littles come forth, my wings are still, I close my eyes and open them and all around are the quivery greentops and the great ball of breath above, I will fly up that high sometime but now I am in a peaceful dawdle that I don't understand, full in the center and sweet heavy in my legs and fluttery of the wingtips, and I lick the air and again and one of these I eat is before me just a dashy-run across the way I ask my center if it wants this bit more and I rise and I rush and this one looks not soft but glinty all over him with the light and he sits on a long-face creature and he makes a sign at me up and down and across

GEORGE

soldier and saint, beheaded by the
Emperor Diocletian, 303

far across the field the evil thing sits, small-seeming from here, my
horse rears and frets sensing the ancient beast as all creatures of God do, while in my ears I still hear the voices of
the villagers *a dragon* they cry, and so it is, I see the evil one
as I have never seen him before, complacent in a meadow
beneath the sun his scaled body the color of a toad his breath
a faint hiss in the air wisps of smoke rising like morning
mist about him the villagers cry *my daughter eaten my son
eaten my husband* and I tell them of the Lord God and his
own son whose body also was destroyed and they cry *that
did us no good* and they wail on and I say *it did you no good
because you have not eaten of your savior* and I kneel before
a priest in a secret place in Rome and I eat the body and
the blood and afterwards I say *father shall I leave my arms*
and he says *fight in the Lord's name* and now I sit on the
edge of this ignorant village and the dragon lifts his head
and unfurls his wings and I thump my fist upon my breast-
plate and I draw my sword and in the center of me there is
only the peace that passes all understanding because of the
things I have eaten

THE
LADY
OF THE
LAKE

enchantress, beheaded by Balin, the
Knight of the Two Swords, circa 470

diving deep I swim in his beard my breath giving out quickly in spite of all I know to do, all that he has taught me, my Merlin, he has schooled me in the things of the pot—the dragon's blood and the mistletoe and the black willow—he has yoked my dreams to my will, he has fed me four poisons—mandrake and henbane and nightshade and his blunt-headed sword, his manthing—he has fed me these till I was safe from each till my skin no longer crawled and my muscles no longer seized and my bones no longer quaked and instead I became strong and cunning and master of the elements and he has shown me how to bare my breasts and my loins and dance silently and I dance while he sleeps and I spin and cry out and he falls deeper into sleep and his staff rolls off his finger-tips and I lift his cloak and he must be dreaming of me for his sword is raised and I put my hand to it and pluck it off—he will enter no other lady now he will live out his life with the memory of me—and it grows in my hand and hardens into steel and its torn root heals into hilt and pommel and I dive deep into my black water where I will wait his summons and I call his sword Excalibur

AH BÁLAM

Mayan ballplayer, beheaded by custom
as captain of losing team, 803

life is held within the ball the lives of all the world's people and the sky
is over us and the high walls are about us with the stone circle
the gateway to heaven fixed there far above and the sun has
swung from low to high as we play for the king and for our
fate for the year to come, the skull of Ah Pitzlaw the Great
is inside the rubber globe so it flies higher today the ring
score is possible, weary I plant my foot and leap and hit the
ball with my hip Ah Mun my brother sliding alongside and
forward to take the next volley of the team of Ah Peku his
small striker catching my volley on the knee and it flies up I
am descended upon my two feet and squaring forward the
ball lifting over my head and Ah Tabai behind me cries like
the macaw and the ball slips low from him past my shoulder
and caroms from the right wall and Ah Peku himself is running already for a mighty hip shot and I see our ancestors
the first men on earth playing ball with the Lords of Death
and even as Ah Peku flies toward the hanging ball I know I
will end headless like the first men, my hands, useless in this
game, tremble, but my heart is ready, the ball flies up and
through the circle

PIERS
GAVESTON

male consort to King Edward II,
beheaded by posse of English nobles, 1312

Edward's gift at my throat my head pushed down rough and I touch my emerald brooch my king gives me emerald and sapphire and ruby we are bright color, he and I, we are fields and sky and pomegranates his mouth smeared with the ruby juice sweet and sharp and I carry his crown soft on a pillow woven of gold, his child-wife put aside for his Piers for his sweet man she watches his crowning like a cameo face of milky glass pinned against a vast cloak of a crowd and I am draped in purple velvet bestarred with pearls the barons also watching us, my Edward and me, they are drops of piss in the king's great sea they push my head roughly down and I touch my emerald hidden in my clothes holding my silken self together my secret smooth stone en cabochon polished round as the tip of the Green Man's member as green as the deep forest, my king and I riding, the heat of my horse the chuff of its breath we are in flight and I am happy my sweet Ed my sweet Ned my sweet Eddy and we run from all the others and night comes and we unbuckle we unbrooch we unburden he says my name and I say his and it is dark and now we are alone in the world we are polished stones we are orbs and scepters

GOOSENECK
(GANSNACKEN)

court jester to Duke Eberhard the Bearded,
beheaded by his master, 1494

quickly, my lord arrives soon, I tether the goat and place the crest of my lord's defeated enemy round its neck and put my oft-merrily-used floppy crown on my ass-eared hat its bells jingling as if in laughter already at my jest and I have secured the rope in the ceiling beam and I stretch and draw myself up, hanging for a moment, breathless from my own wit, my father places his hand on my shoulder and pushes me toward the Duke descended from his horse and laughing at the belt of choked geese around my waist, me wishing to keep their feet dry I say, and he laughs loud and I am excited by this sound, my jokes are my lovers thrilling me, and he takes me to Württemberg and a life of mirth and he will soon be here I begin to swing on the rope, pulling hard at it and I am swinging faster and the goat looks up at me and I wave at him whom I will, as the great Duke, shortly leap upon in antic triumph and the door opens and it is the Duke and I am a jester not a sailor the goat breaks his knot and bolts just as I leap from the rope and fly at my stricken lord and fall heavy upon him, crotch to face, and alas I am already full excited at my joke, like a lover

THOMAS
MORE

Lord Chancellor of England and saint, beheaded
by King Henry VIII for opposing his divorce, 1535

arm around my neck the king leads me out among my roses the Thames sliding heavily along just beyond the rosemary hedge *you never fail me* he says, tugging me closer in the crook of his arm his breath on my face smelling of pheasant and ale from my table *let's speak now of the stars spinning round the earth* he says, and I sit in a palace hall the king and Catherine the queen beside him and the plates are of gold and the servants are backtreading softly and there is not a sound, we wait for Henry's hands to open from the fists beside his plate and the peacocks are before us their bright plumes vanished their flesh darkened by the fire and waiting, the king loosens his right hand and takes up a knife and he places his left hand on the back of the bird and the knife comes down, the body comes apart, and he lifts the meat and he says *eat,* but my hands are folded before me, I am kneeling, I wait—where now?—there is only darkness *eat* I open my mouth *Corpus Domini nostri* his arm is round my neck he twists me to him his hair a fiery crown *I am your king* he says, and it is dark again and I lift my eyes to a body torn *Jesu Christi* the bread on my tongue I eat my king

ANNE
BOLEYN

Queen of England, beheaded after the displeasure
of her husband, King Henry VIII, 1536

tiny and gray is the boy and I am undone, him being no living boy
and no heir to my husband, though I hold his body close and
I am breathless with love for him, and the next is merely a
lump of blood between my legs and he was my last chance
to live, this clot this stain this wet-cleansed spot in my place
of sex, but still there is my sweet girl my Elizabeth her pale
face and her hair the color of the first touch of sun in the sky,
the pale fire of her hair, she turns her gray eyes to me and I
know I am soon to leave her and she is dressed in russet velvet
and a purple satin cap with a caul of gold and the candlelight
thrashes about the walls and I say to her *Lady Princess I will*
always be your mother and she says in her wee voice *madam*
you are my Queen and she bows as she has been taught and I
ache to take her up but she is right, of course, we are who we
are to each other and I am who I am to the man who must
cast me off now, and I say *rise my sweet child* and she straight-
ens and lifts her face and I bend to her, I draw near to her, I
cup my daughter's head in my hands

CATHERINE
HOWARD

Queen of England, beheaded
for adultery by Henry VIII, 1542

what a tumble what a tumble rolling in the sudden dark the secret
parts of my body my own body recently giving forth blood
thick and fragrant and then, soon after, my first Henry,
Henry the First, whose hands I whisper my secrets to who
touches my hidden body my self and what sweet tumblings
roll through me Henry who teaches me the flute I hold in two
hands and blow into his flute and there is music and then the
dark of night in Lambeth my step-grandmother somewhere
far away in another room and I lie dormitoried amidst the
unmarried girls with great unseen puffing all about and
my own Francis, Francis the First, king of the dark, and he
places his secret inside mine and what a tumble it is breaking
me in two and then reuniting me turning me into him, and
Henry my second, eighth to the realm, his body enormous
and folded into hidden places and he has parts only I will
touch, the abscess of his leg issuing forth a pale green flow
do you not find this loathsome he asks, softly for once, *no* I say
it is our secret, and my cousin Thomas whose pepper I am
happy to cull pulled from the deep earth for me to see and it
destroys me at last I walk unsteady to the block has it happened I can't remember I can't see I tumble

LADY JANE
GREY

Queen of England for nine days,
beheaded by Queen Mary Tudor, 1554

I am certain he does love me, my good John Aylmer, who teaches me
Latin and Greek and French and Italian—o cara mio—he
touches with his forefinger that hollow of bone beneath my
throat and he says to me *Jane est omnes divisa in partes tres*
and I am but fourteen years upon this earth when this love
begins when John puts his fingertip beneath my throat and
his face bows slightly and the men ruffle to their knees,
their faces bowed, the crown on my head, and my brocade is
gold and silver—I think only of the dress not of the crown,
which is my husband's desire and his father's—I am not this
tall but for the chopines I totter upon and I settle into the
royal barge and sail upon the dark surface of the river and
all the faces of London look and are silent Edward my king
being dead his head bows and the sound rises from his chest
he touches his mouth and upon his fingertips there is a dark
red bloom and he crosses himself forehead, chest, shoulder,
and then his bloody hand passes across his throat and there
is only one touch upon my throat my sweet John naming
the three parts of Jane: the heart, which I know now is his,
and the body, which has lain down already a voiceless child
upon the earth, and my head

MARY
STUART

Queen of Scots, beheaded
by Queen Elizabeth 1, 1587

dark abrupt the bite at my neck gone, *sweet Jesus* I say the bite fierce
upon me, my breath snarled somewhere in my chest I wait
silent, my sweet Geddon inside my petticoat lays his furry
throat into the bend behind my knee, the cold of the stone
rises to me, hands pressing my shoulders, a veil of Corpus
Christi cloth descends before my eyes, words appear about
forgiveness and innocence and they are from my mouth
though they might as well be from a separated head, his muzzle wetly tracing along my calf Geddon presses his wee body
into my petticoat as I kneel, I stand before the stone block
in the center of the Great Hall the February cold raking my
breasts through my bodice scarlet the color of martyrdom,
men's hands upon me roughly pulling off my gown of black
satin and velvet, my throat naked now, *be gentle with the lamb*
I say as he lifts the golden Agnus Dei off my neck, and my
rosary, Geddon's claws clicking along at my heels I cross the
stone floor refusing the arm of a man, down the great stair-
case my heart beating faster than Geddon's, Fotheringhay's
Great Hall is below me full of upturned faces, I press him
close to me his heart racing against my throat, brushing the
hair from his eyes I say *there now, little man, we must see to go
down these steps*

WALTER
RALEIGH

courtier and explorer,
beheaded by King James 1, 1618

Bess my dear old queen my Elizabeth her lips brittle her body smelling sharply beneath the clove and cinnamon from her pomander she lies next to me in the dark still besmocked though the night is warm and she has asked me here at last and I am masted for her and her bedchamber is black as pitch so she is but a shadow *no torch* she cried as I entered *upon pain of death* and now we are arranged thus my own nakedness perhaps too quick she says *call your new-found land the place of the virgin, Virginia, to honor my lifelong state* and I flinch but her smock does rise and I find the mouth of her Amazon her long fingers scrawling upon my back a history of the world *oh sir oh sir you have found the city of gold at last* she says, knowing me well this fills my sails the jungles of ancient lands are mine my queen *oh swisser swatter* she cries and falls away and I lie beside her staring into the dark, and I am sated certainly, but the moment calls for some new thing, and I say *wait, my queen* and I am out her door to the nearest torch and I have already pre- pared the treasure from my new world, this sweet sotweed this tobacco, and I sail back and slip in beside her and we sit and we smoke

BRITA
GULLSMED

Swedish woman, beheaded
for alleged witchcraft, 1675

night has come and curls about my head and stays and sleeps a long
sleep, for months here on the edge of the taiga I rise to trim
the lamp and Margit leaps silently up and rubs her chin on
my knuckle she is not an imp of Satan my black cat but she
is not of these others either, these humans I am one of, I lie
down in the darkness of my bed and once again there is a
man and I am safely that to the world, the woman beside
him, he lies heavy upon me raking my face with his beard
and beating my loins and cursing the ashen soil he turns and
cursing my barren womb and I am of him he says but I cannot draw a breath and I do not know him and he is gone to
molder in the ground and now Margit leaps upon my chest
and she tramps softly there drooling and murmuring to me
and I lay my hands upon her fur and we purr together and
I am this cat and through her I am the spruce and the pine
standing all about and I am the moon-glint of the ice and
the drifting of the snow and the cry of the wolf and she lays
her face against mine and I am the scattered white fire of the
stars and I am the long long night

LOUIS XVI

King of France, guillotined by order
of the French Revolutionary Tribunal, 1793

thrash and flurry in the undergrowth a bird a boar a stag the rush of wings of legs I lift a Charleville to my shoulder the musket cool to my hands I squeeze the trigger and feel heavily that half heartbeat of silence and then the cry and the kick of her, the night my bed I shudder the trees nearby I am alone at wood's edge *be a man* the king my father says but I am not a man and I feel the beast there invisible in the dark—the Beast of Gévaudan—he is far from Paris but he steps from the woods before me a wolf as big as a lion a hundred dead in the countryside he has passed by the animals of the field to savage a man or woman or child and he faces me and he lifts his ragged muzzle to the sky and howls *liberty to kill, equality of death, fraternity of beasts* and I wake and I am still a child my king's horsemen are off slogging through the marshes of the Auvergne to find him but he is with me and I am king now and I pass the smoking musket to my man who hands me another and I shoot and shoot again and again and the bird falls and the boar and the stag but behind me is the beast and he seizes me by the head

MARIE
ANTOINETTE

Queen of France, guillotined by order
of the French Revolutionary Tribunal, 1793

softly on the arm he touches his wife and they hesitate in the dim
corridor I a few steps behind holding tight to nurse's petticoat and I know how never never again will I be present
in a moment like this because there is always the great
goose-flock of my brothers and sisters and always there are
courtiers and ladies-in-waiting and I am but a little girl a
little little girl with a lute I can play and satin shoes with
such elegant thin soles I feel the cold stone on my toes and
he touches his wife's arm, he who is Emperor of Austria,
King of Jerusalem, Hungary, Bohemia, Dalmatia, Croatia,
and even more, that's as far as I can remember, I am small as
small can be I could crawl into the belly of my lute and stay
there looking between the strings he touches his wife's arm
and he is my father and she is my mother the Empress of
Austria and Queen of Jerusalem and Hungary and so forth
and her skirts are bright and enormous I could live inside
them and bring my three dogs and my pony too and all my
clothes and the skirts are a problem for my father who has
touched my mother's arm because he leans far over far across
them and nearly falls but she turns her face to him knowing
he is her beloved and he kisses her

MARIE-JEANNE
BÉCU
(COMTESSE DU BARRY)

mistress to King Louis xv, guillotined
by order of the French Revolutionary Tribunal, 1793

snow is falling the Seine runs with ice and I come in from the cold
my face tingling I climb the narrow stairs Monsieur Gluck
pushing past me descending and humming some bit of sad
music and I am led by the elbow and now I am beside his
bed, Monsieur Voltaire, and he takes my hand and draws it
to his face and the tip of his long nose touches my knuckle
as his lips kiss my fingers and his breath is labored like my
King I sit beside Louis and I cannot see the pox upon him
in the dark but his breath drags itself heavily through his
body and I bend to him and whisper *my Lord the child you
lately took to your bed has done this to you* and my hand falls
upon his wrist and squeezes hard and Monsieur Voltaire lifts
his face from my hand and there is a faint stain of blood at
the corner of his lip and he narrows his eyes at me *we are
merely at a play, my dear* he says and I ask *is it true there is no
place beyond, where the King will hold me again* and he says
*whether there is a heaven and hell or not, I am afraid you are
finished with Louis* and only as I speak do I understand why
it is I reply *then all is for the best*

ANTOINE-LAURENT

LAVOISIER

scientist, guillotined by order
of the French Revolutionary Tribunal, 1794

air and fire, I breathe deep upon a shore in Brittany and the sun is falling into the sea before my eyes but I am full of thoughts, the ideas of things beyond my sight—the essence of fire is matter fusing with oxygen—a flame from a candle by my bed this vast orb of sun the torch lighting the way past iron doors my wrists shackled my time come my breath guttering like a flame, these are all one, the welter of the sun the welter in my chest, I have proved this also—to burn, to breathe are the same process—the oxygen of the air rushes inside the furnace of my lungs and it flares I give off heat I dress Monsieur Seguin in a suit of taffeta and elastic gum and I seal his mouth with putty and his breath comes and goes through my instruments through my mind he lives he burns we carry our own small sun inside us and not a particle of mass is lost nothing is lost we fuse we are carried off to another state my father-in-law moves ahead of me along the corridor and now he lays down his head on the instrument and the blade falls the head falls one fire goes out and another begins and nothing is lost on a shore in Brittany the sun vanishes but the seams of cloud flare up before me

ANDRÉ
CHÉNIER

poet, guillotined by order
of the French Revolutionary Tribunal, 1794

great the minds in Mother's gilded chairs, Lavoisier and David and
 Suvée, and along the edge of our salon the heavy scent of
 women, lavender and jasmine and the smell of their bodies,
 and the mounting of powdered hair that falls now about
 the shoulders of the Duchess of Fleury who kissed Mother's
 cheeks and me full on the mouth and asked *are you truly a*
 man and *who here is a poet,* dull-eyed now she drifts near our
 jailer who palms her breast and she pauses as if in thought
 and he lets her pass, *Lavoisier is gone to the blade* whispers
 Suvée who has bribed for paints, and I sit for him in a slant
 of light from the high window and he lifts his brush and
 tells me to stop trembling, the stone hall full of our kind our
 lace filthy the turnkeys lifting their red Phrygian caps to
 cheer the reading of tomorrow's condemned, and in my cell
 my hands will not stop quaking nor my chest nor my knees
 when I try to stand and I pace and I wait for my own brush
 my own paint as words pass through my head in a death cart,
 iron wheels turning on the cobbles, they pass to the scaffold
 and are lost, but now: at last, my quill, my ink, a basket full
 of dirty clothes, my words are hid within, *I am* and *I am*

MAXIMILIEN
ROBESPIERRE

lawyer and revolutionary, guillotined
by the Revolutionary Convention, 1794

Father dressed immaculately his knee breeches his silk stockings his tailcoat Mother dead in the parlor her arms folded across her chest he leans against the far wall and I am trying to get my arms around Augustin and Charlotte and Henriette they seem like children to me now, my brother and my sisters, though I am myself only six years on this earth I try to hold them my arms straining and inadequate and I know already that the man leaning there is dead to us too and I am responsible and now the door shuts hard the knocker clangs he has said nothing I follow quickly and strain at the door and he is gone his horse clatters away and he is gone the Bois de Boulogne is full of citizens dressed innocently in tricolor trousers and clogs and red caps I walk among them my hound at my side the summer daylight lingering and they look to me and I want to open my arms they are children and there are many who would harm them and I am in my room above the carpentry yard the sky incarnate with dawn my words prepared at last for the Convention and I dress in white silk stockings and knee breeches and floral waistcoat and black tailcoat and red cravat and my hair is powdered and on the cobbles a scaffold and the blade, dear father, for us all

PIERRE-FRANÇOIS
LACENAIRE

criminal and memoirist,
guillotined for murder, 1836

slim at hip and thigh my lover my fiancée my guillotine but her opening is large, large enough for me to give her everything my head sliding inside her, she is tall and she is painted crimson not mere lips and cheeks but all over my sweet woman—her narrow shoulders, her arms held primly to her side, her lap that I will fling myself upon—all her thin body is rouged for me, all but her bosom which is naked and unadorned, polished bright, her sharp-edged tit that waits for me and has always waited for me, I pass her in the street in a blood dawn and she will soon give herself to another man—she is no virgin, my fiancée, I am reconciled to her past with others—and this first moment I see her I stagger to a stop I am but a boy a petty thief and my father is at my side his mustache waxed into rapier points he lifts his hand toward the lady and says *that is where you will end* and cuffs the back of my head and I am betrothed and I come to her no virgin I put my own blade deep inside a widow she moans though it is but a boy's affair to prepare me for my worldly lover: I stand before her now I bow I slide I enter her and I await her ferocious embrace

TA CHIN

Chinese wife,
beheaded by her husband, 1838

straight and whole are my feet I would rise and run as I have loved
for many winkings of the moon to run with my brothers
but I press my feet side by side and wiggle my toes this last
time and whisper to them *goodbye* I know what is before
me my mother in the courtyard singing prayers to Kuan
Yin the goddess of mercy, not to spare me a life of pain but
to wither my feet to perfection, the mercy of the golden
lotus, the mercy of a wealthy man to keep me, I tremble I
am ready to weep but for these tiny stones of anger Kuan
Yin has placed in the corners of my eyes even as the foot-
binder puts the soaking tub before me that first night even
as my husband trembles before me in the torch light trembling always from the opium but this night he trembles
from what he believes about the brushing of my sleeve by
a man he himself brought to our house and my mother
sings and my toes are seized and folded hard under and the
wrappings wind and wind and squeeze and my arch cracks
and I see Buddha in heaven sitting on his lotus but it is my
naked foot the golden lotus he sits upon and hands push me
down my neck made bare and I cry *please, before my head
cut off my feet*

JACOB

American slave, beheaded
by his owner, 1855

sowbelly frying in the first coming-up light I smell it being only a
child my Sukey-mammy whisper me about how my own
from-her-body mammy done been sold away but she still
loves me the morning bell ringing on some other plantation
far off Sukey-mammy singing *my way's cloudy go send them
angels down* our own morning bell ringing and I am a strong-
back man and the driver beats me bullwhip fire, now across
my right side, now across my left, and another day he beats
me, and another, my back always on fire, clearing some new
part of the forest for corn and for cotton the chopping done
and the grubbing and the log heaps piled and burning filling
the night sky with flame, and I know something burning in
me and Sukey lying in the dirt the driver nudging her at the
shoulder with his boot cause she tell a child how he have a
soul of his own and that night I am rushing and my thumbs
dig deep in the driver's throat and I lay a torch to a hayrick
the sky going hot as a bullwhip lash behind me the hounds
calling and I am running hard through corn row and forest
and I am a child and I walk just a little ways from my Sukey
to the window and I see the first fire of dawn and a bell is
ringing far off somewhere

ANGRY EYES

Apache warrior, beheaded
by Mexican troops, 1880

breechcloth and moccasins only these things on my body and my
head bound by a cloth band my face and chest and arms
stained but I do not know the colors I do not look, my eyes
are fixed on the horizon beyond mesquite and piñon and
stone and I am ready to fight though I have no bow no arrow
not even the rifle, I bend to the white man in dark blue, the
first to die by my hand, and I listen for his spirit nearby, his
hair the color of flame his face filled with tiny faded spots
painted there perhaps to call upon the stars his mouth open
voiceless my arrow through the center of his chest I put my
hand on the stock of his rifle, still listening but there is nothing no bird no insect—*where are you, my foe?*—and the sun
is setting and my hands are empty and I dance, like a woman
I dance with mincing steps my elbows held close against me
my face impassive before the fading light, the edge of the
world is the color of old blood, my body dances stealthily all
my flesh trembling to an unheard drum and I am alone in
this place, but no, his spirit whispers he is beside me now,
in breechcloth and moccasins, and we dance barely moving
nearly touching I and this white man with hair of flame

CHIN CHIN
CHAN

student, beheaded by Chinese authorities for
maintaining a romantic correspondence with an American
girl he met while studying in the USA, 1882

moon no longer a blossom a pearl a lantern in a lover's door but a
bodiless face, mine, in a train window, she on the platform
trying not to look at me directly, as if she were there for
someone else, and the train hurtles in the dark and I stare
into the stars and not even a poet could find the moon in
this sky not even Li Po in a boat with quill and ink in hand
he searches this night sky and then looks at me from across
the water and shrugs and I am the cicada, seventeen at last,
my skin splits open and I emerge a perfect man ready to sing
but there is so little time and the song I hear in return fades
in the grind of these engines, I sit with my own quill and
ink, the cicadas singing in the courtyard outside, *my dear
Elizabeth my love* these words I write blur before my eyes
even as she draws near, the smell of lavender the low trill of
her laughter and then a sigh *you sweet boy what are we to do*
she says and I put my hand on hers and I float above in the
dark and I see Li Po in his boat and he leans far out over the
water opening his arms to embrace the severed head of a
moon and he tips forward and vanishes

DAVE
RUDABAUGH

outlaw and briefly member of Billy the Kid's gang,
beheaded by townspeople in Parral, Mexico, 1886

ready now to throw down on me some old Johnny Reb calls me out
and I'm young and twitchy and into my hand comes my
1860 Colt Army my first sweet thing walnut in my palm
black powder and paper-wrapped cartridges eight-inch bar-
rel coming out and it's been around a long time and knows
what to do the bluing near all rubbed off but you can see
the big-masted ships etched on the cylinder the Texas navy
blowing up the Mexicans their dark faces around me hands
grabbing and a later Colt in my hand my Peacemaker barks
like a stable dog a fat Mex flying back from the table his
sombrero spattered from my bullet in his brain and Billy
touches my shoulder, the Kid is dead but there are his eyes,
as blue as noonday, and his tiny hand on my shoulder, he has
the smallest damn hands, like a girl, Billy whispers *let's ride*
and I lift my hand to touch his and I'm holding my first Colt
all sassy and sweet and long and it thumps and kicks and
goes hot and Johnny Reb is falling backward, my first kill,
and I say to him *here's me,* and all at once I see my life ahead
my hand full of pistol my trigger finger touchy as my cock
and I'm riding hard and I'm lying under the stars and Billy's
sleeping nearby quiet as a girl

AGNES
GWENLAN

factory girl, decapitated by elevator, 1899

quarry sounds, the thump and boom all day, the dishes rattle and Mama flinches each time with Papa out there breaking up the mountain and then he and my uncles are by the fire and they sing and I huddle into sleep *ar hyd y nos* they sing *all through the night* and I am curled on a straw mattress stacked with a hundred others belowdecks the ocean out in the dark all around us and Mama lies above me I can hear her crying for my father crushed by falling slate, a quarryman's death, Miss Liberty watches us sail by, her torch lifted in the twilight, and it suddenly flares into electric light and we gasp and cheer and we sit in the harbor, the city on one hand and Ellis Island on the other, a basket goes over the side and up comes a strange new thing bananas I would eat one skin and all but for a man with quarry hands bending near and peeling it for me and I eat and it is good and he is gone and we are in an open trolley, Mama and I, and we are carried up Broadway beneath buildings higher than mountains and harder than slate and the tenement is dark and surrounds us like the sea and he sings softly in my ear *sleep my love and peace attend thee* and I whisper *all right Papa all right*

CHARLES H.
STUART

Texas farmer, beheaded
by his two teenage daughters, 1904

underfoot the pine board cricks, I pause and let it die, I want to go in quiet, the dark and the chill are coming up under my nightshirt and I'm skittish feeling the dangle of my parts I'm moving along again bobbling and churning down there, the door is closed I come near and I palm the knob which is cool as the curve of their shoulders I turn the knob softly but now they're sitting in sunlight in the kitchen their mama working the water pump in the yard, them both side by side, my daughters, come from my flesh, and Wilhelmina is old enough to look at me that way—the stare that don't flicker—the woman-stare like her mama but without the prattle and the complaints—Valmer not yet with the stare, her eyes still restless like some other women I know—and the pine board cricks under my step and I keep on to the doorknob and I touch it and it's cold and I turn it and the pine board cricks and I slide on along and my hand goes to the doorknob and it is serious cold to the touch—no, not cold at all—it's hot it's searing hot my hand is fixing to torch up but I can't let go and from under the door comes the smell of sulphur and I know it's not them inside, it's what's next for me

ROKHEL

POGORELSKY

Jewish woman, beheaded
in Russian pogrom, 1905

taste of horseradish taste of nettle I draw the covers tight about me the trees beyond the dark window lash in the wind my brother nearby weeps against his will *sorry Papa sorry* and beneath the wind my father's voice tumbles *Pinchas be still the blood was on the doorpost* the lambs in the field raise their head to a hollow sound the soles of my feet quake *our sons were spared* father says to Pinchas but in the field I hear horses and I have my own first son on my back my Aron and I turn from the sound of hooves and I run across the field that rolls beneath me twisting at my ankles I look behind and the men on horses stay on the road a dozen Cossacks in high boots and billowing trousers and one turns his face toward me I run hard and they go on toward the village and I follow the hedge line and through a stand of water oaks and Aron begins to cry his tiny hands plucking at my ears *be still* I say and my cottage now my husband gone a lashing in my chest like trees in a wind and a basket by the step, I put my son inside, my shawl on top, for when this all is done another must find him: a scythe nearby, I cut my hand and spill my blood upon the door

JOHN
MARTIN

boy, decapitated by subway after lifting sidewalk
grate and falling onto the tracks below, 1921

Babe oh Babe hit it all the way out here Babe and jumping jimjams he's done it the ball lifting up like a Fourth of July rocket but not exploding just keeping on going up and coming my way out here in the right-field bleachers and all the Polo Grounds Johnnies around me losing their bowlers falling on themselves and there's a rush from the dark and steel on my throat and the nickel rolls perfect on its edge and we're all real quiet my friends and me and down it goes into the grate and down I go into the dark after it and down I go falling to the track I can get up now but something's happened to my arms and legs they're flimsy loose and too light to lift and it's only jostling shoulders and elbows and sweat beads flying and hats tumbling and I fight clear and Babe's thirty-first of the year is falling from the sky rushing at me oh Babe the orphan boy oh Babe smoking a cigar in his tweedy cap a few weeks ago he comes out of the stadium trailing smoke and I got nothing for him to sign but the back of my hand and this time I'll take him a ball but all of a sudden it dies and falls a few rows in front of me Babe signs my skin and puts his hand on my head

HENRI
LANDRU

second-hand furniture dealer, also known as
the "Bluebeard of Gambais," guillotined for
the murder of ten women, 1922

parlor mirrors are hard to sell when flawed like this one, tinting my beard the color of a bruise, I clap my hand over the bristled hair and turn to this woman but her deer's eyes are blind to my beard, seeing only my sympathetic gaze, and her face is traced with age and her upper lip is furred and her husband is long dead and her hands are brittle from scrubbing and she is worse than dead as a widow, her money useless to her, the newspapers were right I am spinning from Mother Goose's mouth—the young wife choking back her disgust at my blue beard, which, however, I do not shave, and I go off giving her all the chateau's keys and warning her on pain of death not to enter the cellar room, the room where I have secretly placed the disassembled bodies of seven wives, the room that yields only to this small key, which, however, I do not simply withhold from her—my hands quicken I kiss Madame's furred lip and she cries out in pleasure and the deal is struck, a moment of passion she would never have had, for the dead man's settee and his four-poster bed and his commode and his wife's head lying upon its pillow and this cleaver in my hand and I cut through and hold it up, her eyes still blinking, and I kiss her trembling lips

PAUL
GORGULOFF

Russian immigrant to France, guillotined
for assassinating French President Paul Doumer
at charity book signing, 1932

silver rivets all around I step into the rocket Paul Gorguloff space pilot who turns to Professor Oberth and shakes his hand I am to fly his rocket to the moon and I step from the rocket the rivets scorched black and great crowds of people press in crying *tell us your story* and I sit before the window and I take up my fine pen and the pistol is on my desk and a sheaf of blank paper and I post the cap of my Mont Blanc and I write *Memoirs of Paul Gorguloff* and the pages tumble from me Paul Gorguloff the writer paces the floor the carpet worn through the desk overflowing I am in a crowd now that clamors for books and they are fools not recognizing the greatness moving among them my pen clipped in my shirt pocket and Claude Farrère—a novelist unworthy to wipe my dripping nib—sits signing and I deign to buy his *Useless Hands* about breadmakers in the distant future replaced by robot hands and he autographs my book with a cheap pen and I turn the book and I uncap my Mont Blanc before his eyes and I sign it above his name *Paul Gorguloff the man who killed the President of the French Republic* Paul Doumer at another table signing his books thinking himself a writer and the pistol is in my hand and I critique his work

BENITA
VON BERG

German baroness, beheaded
by Adolf Hitler for espionage, 1935

dying tip of one cigarette I touch to another, my cell at Plötzensee is full of tobacco smoke and I fill my lungs holding very still, woolen socks on my feet prison trousers and shirt if I could but whiten my face and trace my lips in scarlet we lean together and sing Brecht the club full of smoke and bodies the emcee in tails and white tie points at me—*welcome to Kabarett madam but free that red fox about your neck he is our comrade*—and it is Munich now a woman in a swirl of silk, her body naked beneath, she leaps onto our table and her womansmell fills my lungs I leave my cigarette in my mouth my hand falling the sound of weeping from some other cell I slip my hand inside these rough trousers to my own cleft like hers flashing above me on the table and her face is white her lips scarlet and Friedrichstrasse is ablaze with electric light passing in a cab his clumsy Polish hand between my legs I whisper *Captain, your country is in danger,* as if I loved him, and our voices swell through the smoke and we sing *there was a time and now it's all gone by* and I move down the corridor into the room of the ax and the executioner turns to greet me and he is dressed in tails and white tie *welcome*

NGUYEN VAN

TRỈNH

Viet Minh guerrilla leader, guillotined
by French Colonial authorities, 1952

very still, I hold my rifle hard against my chest and I am careful
even in the breath I draw I am folded against a mangrove
tree my knees tucked close I move my eyes but I can see
none of my comrades and of course I cannot hear them for
we all wait on the noisy French wait till they are between
the two columns of us and I should at least be able to see my
friend Ky I know his place forward in a closing of vines but
he is not there and I wait for the French and I think of my
father in his collar and cravat and the way his head would
draw down like a tortoise when he spoke of the French-
man who ran his lycée *pull your collar off, my father, seize
by the throat that man who shames you* and my father is a
vase of ashes and my mother prays in the bourgeois myth
that his spirit lives yet in another realm, and I hear them
nearby, breaking dry leaves beneath their feet, and it is time
and I make a sharp bird cry and I leap now but there is no
rifle in my hands I have come from the trees onto the path
and these are not Frenchmen but Vietnamese in mandarin
dress and one turns his face and it is my father and he offers
his hand

ALWI
SHAH

Yemeni executioner, beheaded
for a crime unrelated to his work, 1958

rising slow from a low place I see a row of heads sitting before me on a stone wall ear-to-ear arrayed beyond my sight to either side, I face them and their eyes turn to me and I hear the stirring of feet all around me, a jumbled huddling-in of bodies naked and battered with bones cracked and bulging knots and blooms of bruise and crusted lappings of blood, how I loved you all, loved righteously snapping the cords of all your lives, and so you come to taunt me but praise Allah I have done his holy work and I took as his sign the trill of sweetness that came upon me in this my work and now I turn and look into the stone-shattered face of Haleema Alsakkaf an adultering woman and she holds in her right hand the head of Akram Alshami her lover who, like the others, moves his eyes to me and I say *praise Allah you have paid righteously* and she says *praise Allah who we call the one God and who loves his creatures, we are sent as you knew us but we are restored in heaven* and I see now that my own head hangs in her left hand and I cry *praise Allah he will have mercy on me also* and she says *the mercy of God seeks sinful love before righteous hatred* and I wait for my head to fall

CHICKEN

Americauna pullet, beheaded
in Alabama for Sunday dinner, 1958

little grit things in the straw here and I peck and peck and they're gone and I go over there a wormy thing but it's a leaf stem which I always grab but it never goes mush like an actual worm which I look and look and listen for and the flying ones come down and they walk among us and they cock their heads and hear the slither in the earth and they grab and up one comes but after a rain it's good for me the worms come up and I run here and I run there and I eat and the grit is good too over there I go for grit though the soft slither is even better but it's dry now dry all around and they are vanished, wait, wait, the rest of me is gone and from beyond the wire from past the dog-leap from down the long ruts I can hear a muttery cluckering and it is like when I broke at last from the eggy wall and into the light and a fluff of feathers hovered near and made this same sound but this muckery wuckering is vast, this at last is the hen who fills the sky, and I am rushing now along the path and the clucking is for me and it is very loud and a great wide road is suddenly before me and she is beyond and I cross

VERA JAYNE

PALMER
(STAGE NAME, JAYNE MANSFIELD)

actress, decapitated in car crash, 1967

faint his face his eyes but I feel the soft run of his hand on my hair I am so tiny I am so much his little Vera that I am breathless I put my arms across his chest my father and I listen to the draw of his breath and he is gone and I am before these faces upturned I could open my arms and not get round them all I am their Jayne I am their Miss Freeway I am their Miss Electric Switch and Miss Photoflash and Miss Geiger Counter I am their Miss Pure Maple Syrup I am the wide clean road to where they want to go and I am the thing you touch to turn on the light and I am the bright caught moment and I am the crackle of invisible fire that will burn the very flesh from your bones and I am sweet beyond all bearing and pure and I am Chanel Number Five I sit in the quiet in a dressing room before the eyes will turn to me and I touch the scent to my skin and suddenly I am the smell of jasmine and of orange blossom and if you concentrate harder I am rose and iris and lily-of-the-valley and if you wait I am amber and patchouli and vanilla and he puts his face in my hair and he breathes in and he says *how sweet*

LE VAN

KY

Hue city official, beheaded
by North Vietnamese troops, 1968

blossoms floating on the Perfume River plumeria and mango and lychee the water itself smelling of mountain flowers even after the blossoms have eddied away I drag my hand in the river my father pulling at the oar and he says my name sharply *Ky* and I take up my own oar again and now we loll in the sun beside the South China Sea my father sleeping my mother huddling against my sister and speaking low and I wander away back toward the river far along the edge of the lagoon and even though there is no one in sight my heart is already beating furiously and the jungle closes in and around a bend she is crouched by the river's edge and I cut toward the tree line before she knows to look up, I circle and I creep close, her back is to me and she must be a peasant girl her skin is dark from the sun and her shirt clings to her, her naked back shines through the thin wet cloth, and she angles her head and pours the river into her long midnight hair, once, and again, and she has stolen my breath and she sits back and shakes her wet hair and I watch, never seeing her face, then she rises and goes away forever, and I understand: though the blossoms pass along in the current and vanish the river still smells sweet

KIMITAKE

HIRAOKA

(PEN NAME, YUKIO MISHIMA)

Japanese novelist, beheaded at his own request by a
paramilitary colleague as he committed ritual disembowelment
after failing to persuade Japan's Self-Defense Forces
to overthrow the government, 1970

Tokyo roiling in flames like the sea my young man's body too frail to find a patriot's death I am a watcher shaping words already from the roof of the arsenal my wrists thin my arms a girl's arms the American bombers invisible in the scarlet smoke of the night sky, the flames now inside my body, brought there by my own hand, my own sword, my samurai arm—no, vanished now—no body at all—but words, always words, only words, which are my coward's sword—and I call the flames to return, to fill the sky with bombs, take the salary-men sleeping on commuter trains take the shops filled with breakfast cereal and French perfume and vacuum cleaners take the politicians who yield our swords, who make our Emperor the English queen, rise up, my country grown girlish and frail, my face grows hot from the flames of Tokyo and from shame at my body and then ten thousand confrontations before a gymnasium mirror and my arms thicken my thighs muscled carrying me to an act, I am breathless with power the rising sun tied round my head I stand before our warriors, our past, and they laugh at a girlish boychild and the city lies quiet against the night the horizon filling not with flame but with words, with manu-scripts, I have named myself after snow I have been cold all along I am only a writer

ROBERT
KORNBLUTH

senior partner in advertising firm,
decapitated by elevator, 1984

look I cry: SHE CLOSED, THE DOOR, RIGHT IN YOUR FACE, THE WHISKERS SIR, YOU MUST ERASE, BURMA SHAVE swept by my headlights, *there, I wrote those words,* my hands clenched tight on the wheel, the wrong thing to say she is quiet beside me quaking and weeping in rage and I yearn for a no more tears formula, *I give the best to you each morning* I say *it takes a wife to know the difference between Hanes and just underwear,* surely I'm not speaking these words to Anne the long-suffering Anne my wife once my wife long ago we are in a brand new 1952 Packard—ask the man who owns one—long before this present darkness came upon me—is it possible? panties more comfortable than wearing nothing?—Anne naked by the window in a luxury suite, affordable comfort, *no more tears* I say, *do you know me* she says, *what we have is the real thing* I say, and she is gone I dream of her and she is wearing her Maidenform Bra and my mouth brims with words that I know will do only harm—would you offer a Tiparillo to a lady?—a cigarette at least, outside the lawyer's office, mellow, an aid to digestion, we smoke and we stay silent and she sighs and is gone, DON'T LOSE, YOUR HEAD, TO GAIN A MINUTE, YOU NEED YOUR HEAD, YOUR BRAINS ARE IN IT

JENNIFER
HADLEY

marketing director,
decapitated in car crash, 1989

overhead jet engines the phone rings and a flash of landing lights outside, the chocolate mint still on my pillow, I know who it is, *hello* I say, *hello* he says, *I'm just down the hall* he says, *I know* I say, *are we going to do this* he says, a statement, my husband has called already to say goodnight and I say *your wife's call, just finished* he says, I don't say that I'm having trouble holding the phone to my ear I am so weak in the limbs breathless, overhead jet engines the phone rings a flash of light beyond the window a jet rushing back to earth from somewhere the chocolate on my pillow *hello* I say, *hello I'm just down the hall* he says, *I know* I say, *are we going to do this* he says, the phone rings a sound like ice falling from the eaves jet engines overhead my husband standing thigh-high in snow just beyond our patio his breath pluming and ice falling between us and then he waves *did it snow* I ask him tonight, *yes* he says *but the ice is worse the wires are down there is no electricity no heat,* I say *goodnight,* the line rasping with his thrown kiss, I put the receiver in the cradle, I pick up the chocolate I put it down, jet engines overhead the phone rings there is a knock at my door

NICOLE BROWN
SIMPSON

California woman,
decapitated by assailant, 1994

running hard along Venice Beach the clutch of breakers around my
feet I run against the pull and I've come to this, to a place
of jasmine smell and sea and car exhaust and stucco walls
and Hollywood spelled across a mountain, and I run easily
with the question *what can I be,* I've got great legs he says,
and he should know because he runs for a living I love to see
him run though he says I don't really understand but I do I
run with him each time he holds something private in his
arm and all the others rush to bring him down but he cuts
and jukes and surges: run now, my children, run down the
hall and close your doors because I cannot, his sweet slick
child's face in the faces of my children, such beautiful skin I
draw my hand tender along his cheek and he closes his eyes
the moon out there rising I am large with her inside me, my
child, and glass shatters and the bones of my face vibrate and
my teeth all hurt I draw my hand along my cheek I think to
try to run and he rushes up fast and I can see what's tucked
there in the crook of his arm and it is me, it is my head, and
I stare into my own eyes and I know the answer always was
his wife

MOHAMMED AZIZ
NAJAFI

Iraqi Shiite cleric, beheaded
by Saddam Hussein, 1996

barren ground but holy, this plateau before me, trampled smooth by the feet of millions, the true people of Allah, but empty now though it is Hajj and the Mount of Mercy is behind me I feel its press between my shoulder blades and the pilgrims should be everywhere but the ground is beaten into silence and there is no one—*oh Allah leave me not alone*—for I have no seed but your holy words, I have no family but the family of your great people, no child but your revealed way, I would summon the millions cloaked in white so I could be among them and we would cry out as one *Allah I have responded to you* I am draped in seamless cotton I am barefoot and I am penitent, and the echo of my prayers is still in my head I have been silent only the briefest of moments and I yearn for the tumult of my brothers in Allah I would kneel and touch my face to this long-beaten ground as one with a million other faces, but no, I am standing upright and I am alone and before me now there is only a desert tamarisk, feathery pink, the merest growing thing and it catches the sun as if it is on fire and I hear a voice say to me *it is time now to take thy only son and cut his throat*

LYDIA
KOENIG

Chicago woman, decapitated
by her son, 1999

baby Mama calls me baby on my lap a lump of cloth baby doll and
then a freckled face, Howdy Doody baby, I hum his name
his puppet strings folded under, not a doll but I like his
hard legs and arms beneath his clothes like real bones, Lake
Michigan at twilight the color of tarnished brass a hand
inside my lap and he asks me that night atop the Prudential
Building the lake too dark to see and then my baby my own
baby boy his bones deep and untouchable inside him, I dress
him in pink thinking it makes no difference I hold him baby
and then in plaid and he has freckles on his nose and he
stinks of urine from his bed I carry the great lump of soiled
cloth and the Tide waiting, the cleaning power of Tide and
Oxydol and Clorox, and the man is gone and my baby cries
all night through, though he is no baby he is returned and
he says *help me find a vein help me tap this vein* and I cannot,
I take his load of piss sheets to the Maytag in the basement
and it is cool here and smells of the lake on a bad day and I
wash them and dry them sitting in the dimness of the basement and I hold these sheets in my lap my baby my baby's
voice is behind me

CLAUDE

MESSNER

homeless man, decapitated by Amtrak train
after laying his neck on the track, 2000

no oh no not him again from the rush of a fucking train I get the old man, what's taking that goddam train so long it was here a moment ago, maybe it's lying on its side jumped by a penny on the track I hide in the weeds and my shiny Lincoln-head is out there waiting for the Illinois Central from Chicago and I know I should be thinking about the careening of the engine the flight of the baggage car into the trees but all I've got is him whipping off his belt to do me, the sonofabitch, he disappears for a week only to come back for this, and I can't fucking believe I'm lifting my hand trying to take his, we're walking along storefronts I'm barely taller than the fire plugs and I'm trying to take that hand and it flicks like at a house-fly, and later on there's a long while, a few years, of just me and my mother and she likes her young man she runs her finger through the great front wave of my hair, and then he's back and he's about breaking my arm and I'm in a barber's chair and I can see my beautiful duck's ass of a do in the mirror and I whisper to the barber *please just a little around the edges* and my dad says *buzz him, buzz him up clean, take it all off*

LOIS
KENNERLY

systems analyst, beheaded in collapse of the south
tower of the World Trade Center, 2001

oh my god oh my god Paul Anka is looking at me now even as he sings he bends down from the stage and his hand comes out asking me to rise to go up there with him and I am next to him dazzled by the lights the crowd roaring his voice near my face *squeeze me oh so tight* and his arm comes around me I am sixteen and now I am twenty and we step out the side door of the church hall and no one has noticed us go, me in my bridal dress and Sam in his tux, and we crouch flat-footed near the door like you see the Vietnamese do on TV and we smoke and I've just married him but this is the moment I know I love him for sure, us smoking outside alone, and the snow is falling beyond my window I have awakened and I know it's time for my baby she's ready though my water hasn't broken and I'm not in any pain I know this is the day and it's still snowing beyond the hospital window the flakes look big as her hands and she's taking my milk and Sam is singing *you're having my baby* and I think him a damn fool, she's mine, and I can hardly see, the lights are so bright, and an arm slips around my waist *put your head on my shoulder*

ISIOMA
OWOLABI

woman of Bani, Burkina Faso,
beheaded by fatwa, 2002

Mother I cannot see your face I walk beside you too young to veil my own but I yearn for your eyes, surely I can see my mother's eyes even in public, let the men turn their own eyes away for my sake, but behind us are the nine mosques that have risen from the earth and their veined walls are beneath our feet, the desiccated road, for father takes us east to a purer love of Allah, and his back is to me—no—he has turned round, in Nigeria, I am nearly a woman, the veil drops upon my face, he whispers that I live now where the road has ended on the cliff's edge and if I lift this thing between me and the world I will lose my balance and fall to my death, so my mother will never see my eyes again in sunlight, and there is a great rushing about me now, she lies dead and veiled and I slip into the night and the moonlight falls upon my naked eyes, my hand in the hand of a man whose body is unveiled and his part rises like a mosque of Bani, and I speak to the world a gentle truth about the prophet and the dark swims upon me I hurtle back along the road to the mosques of my home where I know that heaven is simply a shaping of the earth

HANADI TAYSEER
JARADAT

law student, beheaded by self-detonation
of shaheed-belt suicide bomb, 2003

I am heavy with child praise Allah I am at last with child my head is full of the law that I am permitted to study to serve our people but I have not forgotten my greater destiny praise Allah I am also with child, the words of the Prophet—peace be upon him—saying *Paradise lies at the feet of mothers,* I have not forgotten, I move across rubbled ground and my baby is pressed hard against my womb wait wait my face is naked my head is bare I touch where my baby is and he is very heavy ten kilos and his bones are large and hard and stacked side by side his cord winds secretly into the pocket of the jeans that bind my legs my loins I wear the clothes of harlots my hand is on his private part I am but to press there, my baby placed in me by a man with his face covered I turn my head and open my cloak to a man I do not know, an angel of Allah surely, his arms around me and my baby is suddenly holding me tight I am moving in a room full of people cursed by Allah my baby heavy against me surely he has eyes and a mouth and a heart, a woman nearby damned but large with child, I have my own, I touch him and he cries out

EARL

DAGGETT

laid-off Mississippi heavy-equipment operator,
beheaded by his lover's husband, 2003

Elmer, that economy-size coon turd who is my friend, points his shotgun straight up over his dang head—and mine, if you please, I'm standing right next to him—and he goes and does this so fast I ain't got time to jump away from sharing his rightly earned fate, he pulls the trigger fixing to kill a squirrel and instead of bringing buckshot and tree limbs and small-animal guts raining down on our heads, like ought to be the outcome, he plumb misses the whole tree and falls backwards—he's got that bad a damn aim—and likewise his thumbs is always about hammered to pulp whenever it's time to tarpaper his barn or fix a porch plank, and he don't even deserve the love of Maisie who has billowy warm thighs and Elmer probably can't even manage to get it into her honey pot, not with both hands on his pecker and a red flag flying between her legs, so I figure I'm okay as I open one eye and it's only half past two and he should be at the planing mill and Maisie is still snoring like a rotary saw beside me and I jump up and grab my pants to make one clean leap: here I go right now I am so light and graceful like a greyhound at the track I'll just leap through that window and be clean plumb away from his ax

MAISIE

HOBBS

Mississippi woman,
beheaded by her husband, 2003

night that's dark as fresh tar on the county road we roll through our trailer park late from Wednesday church and I rest my chin on our Chevy's door and one lit window after another goes by Mandy Lou leaning into Henry him putting his arms around her and shadows going up and down beside the flicker of Lila's TV and I'm thinking I'm fixing to grow up and take a man inside me and I'm moving along in another tarry night through the woods out back of Stanco's Lawn Ornaments and Tombstones and he's got me by the hand saying sweet things like *you little dual-exhaust you, you little road-runner let me rev you up* and I keep on batting at him till we're on a stump at the quarry pond and this is the good part this is the part I knew I'd like, the cuddle beforehand, him knowing I'll say yes and it makes him cuddle real good cause I told him already it's the only way he's getting inside me and I say I got to have a great kiss first and then he can go down there to what he wants and he squares around and puckers and he moves in fast glancing off my nose and sliding along my cheek and he says *oopsie doops sorry there Maisie* and I say *that's okay Elmer* he's so cute being clumsy I know I'll marry him

ROBERT
DURAND

commuter, beheaded in crash
of Staten Island ferry, 2003

underneath her earlobe with its wisp of invisible fuzz the cleavage
of her toes in her pointiest black stilettos the hollow of her
ankle her sacral dimples each holding a tiny shadow as she
sleeps in the morning light that slides beneath the shade,
unawares she has sloughed off the toga of bedclothes the
long indent of her spine bared and those dimples I put the tip
of my tongue in one and she stirs, my wife, her shoulders her
tall knuckles the lift of her arm the hollow beneath I put my
face there and she bats at my ear *I'm not fresh* she says, *it's you*
I say, kissing this hidden place, the round forward points of
her hips that I palm as she sits upon me, my wife, my Ann,
and she will not close her eyes *I want to see you in that moment*
she says the knot of her wrist her brow I ruffle her brow with
my lower lip the tiny arc of a scar on the back of her hand the
mark of a Christmas-tree light the bruises of that childhood
long gone and the father dead and the mother too just this
scar remains and I turn her hand and I kiss her there and she
puts her hands on my cheeks and she draws me to her and
presses me down and she kisses me on the top of the head

TYLER
ALKINS

civilian truck driver, beheaded
by the Iraqi Al-Tawhid Wal-Jihad (Monotheism
and Holy Struggle) group, 2004

my name is Tyler Alkins my voice sounding far off guttering like the bleeder flames in the refineries outside Houston *my mother's name is Marietta* the red dot on the video camera a drop of blood at the corner of her mouth *my father's name is Ralph* and the old man is upon me grabbing at my shoulder *boy turn around and take this beating now* he says but I wrench my mind to him and me out with shotguns waiting for the doves to break and then he squeezes at my shoulder, but gently, the feathers of a dove fluttering still from the air the kick of the gun shuddering through me and a hand comes upon my shoulder from behind and a voice cries *allahu akbar* and it is just me and my rig driving the interstate hard at night the sodium vapor lamps coming up out of the dark like a sky full of nearby stars *I live in Lubbock Texas* and our own George is the President and he calls upon all of us and I can drive a truck and my old man grabs my shoulder and I have done something wrong and he says *in the name of Jesus* and a bite at my neck *allahu akbar* and George has prayed to God and he will kick ass and plenty of it and my father cries *take this beating now for your own good*

VASIL
BUKHALOV

Bulgarian agricultural aid worker, beheaded
by the Iraqi Salafist Brigade of Abu Bakr al-Siddiq, 2004

on my tongue the bitter bite of green walnut Baba's face in the lamp light her hands black from the peeling of the skins the nuts inside white and very soft, too young yet to be hardened, and I eat another and another until bitter is sweet to me and the cheese she gives me is soft as well and tastes like the goat's milk but after it's turned and it tastes also of the stable floor and of the rutted earth and I make a face I am very young and Baba puts her hand on mine and she says *eat more and you will find the taste is good* and then her hand touches my face *you look like your grandfather in this light* and I have seen a picture on a postcard of Diado and I will look again to see if I can find my own face and I look into my own son's face and see Diado's eyes and I make cheese and I grow pears and I give my son a curl of cheese from my fingertip and he makes a sour face and Baba lays her forearm beneath the piss-spill of the lamp and she shows me the number there, faint, in blue, *I was in Macedonia because of your grandfather and they took us* and this is all she says and we eat bitter herbs and they taste sweet to me now

ROBERT OLEN
BUTLER

writer, decapitated on the job, 2008

heedless words but whispered, they begin as I stand before the guillotine and I am filled with the scent of motor exhaust and wood fire and fish sauce and jasmine in a strange country, a good scent, her hand in mine at last, the city that roars in my dreams is beyond the stucco walls a balcony the Saigon River the rim of the world bleeding from the setting sun and self-righteousness, the guillotine in the museum rises above the cannon barrels and rotor blades and unexploded bombs the blade darkened by the wet air and the voices begin to speak not in my head not in the place where I think but in my ear directly in my fingertips a computer screen before me the clatter of keys like tiny clawed feet running in a wall, come to me little ones nibble from my hands snuggle into my pockets and curl your naked tails in peace like these words already fixed and bound and tucked beneath my arm, half a dozen autographs signed tonight and thanks for buying my book I step into the elevator and I am alone and the air buzzes in silence and I consult the scrap of paper in my pocket to see where I belong and I push the button and down the hall there are voices agitated ardent full of yearning and I lean forward and I stick my head out to listen

HEADS

MUD, man	Northern Europe	ca. 40,000 B.C.
MEDUSA, Gorgon	Greece	ca. 2000 B.C.
Marcus Tullius CICERO, politician	Rome	43 B.C.
JOHN the BAPTIST, prophet	Roman Empire	ca. 30
Valeria MESSALINA, empress	Rome	48
DIOSCORUS, shipmaster	Pontiole	67
PAUL, apostle	Rome	67
MATTHEW, apostle	Ethiopia	78
VALENTINE, priest	Rome	ca. 270
DRAGON, beast	Libya	301
GEORGE, soldier	Palestine	303
The LADY of the LAKE, enchantress	Britain	ca. 470
AH BALAM, Mayan ballplayer	Mexico	803
Piers GAVESTON, royal consort	England	1312
GOOSENECK, court jester	Germany	1494
Thomas MORE, Lord Chancellor	England	1535
Anne BOLEYN, Queen	England	1536
Catherine HOWARD, Queen	England	1542
Lady Jane GREY, Queen	England	1554
Mary STUART, Queen of Scots	England	1587
Walter RALEIGH, courtier	England	1618

Brita GULLSMED, woman	Sweden	1675
LOUIS XVI, King	France	1793
Marie ANTOINETTE, Queen	France	1793
Marie-Jeanne BÉCU, mistress	France	1793
Antoine-Laurent LAVOISIER, scientist	France	1794
André CHÉNIER, poet	France	1794
Maximilien ROBESPIERRE, revolutionary	France	1794
Pierre-François LACENAIRE, criminal	France	1836
TA CHIN, wife	China	1838
JACOB, slave	USA (GA)	1855
ANGRY EYES, Apache warrior	Mexico	1880
Chin Chin CHAN, student	China	1882
Dave RUDABAUGH, outlaw	Mexico	1886
Agnes GWENLAN, factory girl	USA (MA)	1899
Charles H. STUART, farmer	USA (TX)	1904
Rokhel POGORELSKY, woman	Russia	1905
John MARTIN, boy	USA (NY)	1921
Henri LANDRU, furniture dealer	France	1922
Paul GORGULOFF, assassin	France	1932
Benita VON BERG, baroness	Germany	1935
Nguyen Van TRINH, guerrilla leader	Vietnam	1952

Alwi SHAH, executioner	Yemen	1958
CHICKEN, Americauna pullet	USA (AL)	1958
Vera Jayne PALMER, actress	USA (LA)	1967
Le Van KY, city official	Vietnam	1968
Yukio MISHIMA, novelist	Japan	1970
Robert KORNBLUTH, advertising executive	USA (NY)	1984
Jennifer HADLEY, marketing director	USA (CT)	1989
Nicole Brown SIMPSON, woman	USA (CA)	1994
Mohammed Aziz NAJAFI, Shiite cleric	Iraq	1996
Lydia KOENIG, woman	USA (IL)	1999
Claude MESSNER, homeless man	USA (IL)	2000
Lois KENNERLY, systems analyst	USA (NY)	2001
Isioma OWOLABI, woman	Burkina Faso	2002
Hanadi Tayseer JARADAT, law student	Israel	2003
Earl DAGGETT, heavy-equipment operator	USA (MS)	2003
Maisie HOBBS, woman	USA (MS)	2003
Robert DURAND, commuter	USA (NY)	2003
Tyler ALKINS, truck driver	USA (TX)	2004
Vasil BUKHALOV, aid worker	Bulgaria	2004
Robert Olen BUTLER, writer	USA (FL)	2008